P9-BTM-771

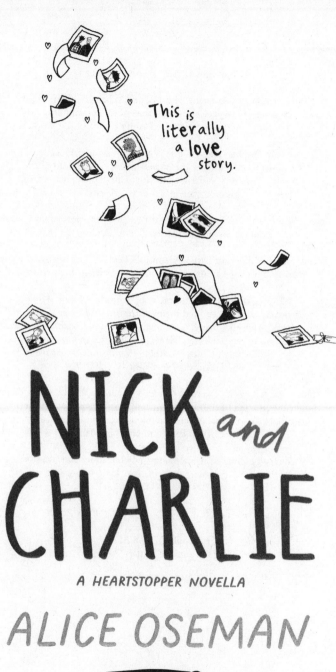

This is
literally
a love
story.

NICK and CHARLIE

A HEARTSTOPPER NOVELLA

ALICE OSEMAN

Scholastic Press / New York

Copyright © 2023 by Alice Oseman

Published by arrangement with HarperCollins Children's Books,
a division of HarperCollins Publishers Ltd. The author asserts
the moral right to be identified as the author of this work.

All rights reserved. Published by Scholastic Press,
an imprint of Scholastic Inc., *Publishers since 1920*. SCHOLASTIC,
SCHOLASTIC PRESS, and associated logos are trademarks and/or
registered trademarks of Scholastic Inc.

Originally published in English in Great Britain by HarperCollins Children's
Books, a division of HarperCollins Publishers Ltd.

The publisher does not have any control over and does not assume any
responsibility for author or third-party websites or their content.

No part of this publication may be reproduced, stored in a
retrieval system, or transmitted in any form or by any means, electronic,
mechanical, photocopying, recording, or otherwise, without written
permission of the publisher. For information regarding permission,
write to Scholastic Inc., Attention: Permissions Department,
557 Broadway, New York, NY 10012.

This book is a work of fiction. Names, characters, places, and incidents
are either the product of the author's imagination or are used fictitiously, and
any resemblance to actual persons, living or dead, business establishments,
events, or locales is entirely coincidental.

Library of Congress Cataloging-in-Publication Data available

ISBN 978-1-338-88510-1

10 9 8 7 6 5 4 3 2 1   23 24 25 26 27

Printed in the U.S.A.   37
First edition, January 2023

YA
Ose

"Yes, very indifferent indeed," said Elizabeth, laughingly. "Oh, Jane, take care."

"My dear Lizzy, you cannot think me so weak, as to be in danger now?"

"I think you are in very great danger of making him as much in love with you as ever."

— Jane Austen, *Pride and Prejudice*

one

CHARLIE

As Head Boy of Truham Grammar School, I've done many things. I got drunk on the wine at parents' evening. I've been photographed with the mayor three times. I once accidentally made a Year 7 cry.

But none of that was quite as bad as having to stop everyone in Year 13 from enjoying their final day of school, which is what our head teacher, Mr. Shannon, is trying to make me do right now.

It's probably worth mentioning that my boyfriend of two years, Nick Nelson, is one of those Year 13s.

"You don't mind, do you?" Mr. Shannon leans on the common-room table where I'm supposed to be revising for my exams but am actually watching Mac DeMarco concerts on my phone. "It's all got a bit out of hand and I think they'd be more likely to listen to you than me, if you see what I mean."

"Erm . . ." I shoot a look at my friend Tao Xu, who's sitting next to me eating a packet of Galaxy Minstrels. He raises his eyebrows at me as if to say, *Sucks to be you.*

I don't really want to say yes.

Year 13's final day of school is *High School Musical* themed. They've hung a giant *East High* sign over the Truham one at the school gate. They've been playing the soundtrack on classroom computers, so wherever you are in the school you can hear a *High School Musical* song playing from somewhere, but you're never quite sure where. They participated in a "What Time Is It" flash mob on the football field at breaktime. And they

4

have all turned up to school either in red basketball outfits or cheerleader outfits. Disappointingly, Nick went for basketballer.

To top it all off, on a non-*HSM*-related note, they've built a fort out of cardboard boxes on the tennis courts and are having a barbeque inside it.

"I just want them to put the barbeque out," says Shannon, obviously detecting how reluctant I am to walk into a box fort of one hundred and fifty people older than me and tell them to stop having fun. "You know. Health and safety stuff. If someone gets burnt, I'll be the one dealing with angry parents."

He chuckles. Mr. Shannon has come to trust me completely over the several months I have been Head Boy. This is hilarious because I rarely do anything he tells me to do.

Keep the teachers on your side and the students on your side. Don't make enemies or too many friends.

That's my advice for getting through school.

"Yeah, sure, no problem," I say.

"You're an absolute life saver." He points a finger at me as he walks away. "Don't revise too hard!"

Tao looks at me, still shoving chocolate into his mouth. "You're not actually gonna go confront the Year 13s, are you?"

I laugh. "Nah. I'll just go see what they're up to and tell them to watch out for Shannon."

My other friend, Aled Last, looks up at me from the opposite side of the table. He's been color-coding his maths revision notes for the past hour. "Can you bring me back a burger?"

I stand up from my chair and put my blazer on. "If there's any left."

The Year 12s have already left for study leave and the only reason I'm here is because I revise better at school than at home. Tao and Aled thought the same. None of us really want to be here, though. It's the hottest day we've had this year and I just sort of want to lie down somewhere with an ice pack on my head.

Nick and I have plans for this weekend. He's finally free from school, and I'm taking a weekend off revision. It's Thursday today; I'm staying over at his tonight. Tomorrow night we're going to Harry's party for everyone in sixth form. Saturday we're going to the beach. Sunday we're going to London.

Not that we don't spend every weekend together anyway.

Not that we don't see each other every single day.

If you'd told me three years ago I'd be in a two-year-long relationship by the time I was seventeen, I would have laughed in your face.

"CHARLIE SPRING!"

As I walk through the box-fort entrance underneath a banner that says *WILDCATS!* Harry Greene approaches me, arms outstretched. He is wearing a twelve-year-old's *High School Musical* cheerleader costume and is exposing a lot more thigh than is probably appropriate for school.

The fort is huge—they've taken over two tennis courts. Along with the hilarious amount of cardboard, they've also stolen at least ten tables from various classrooms and have a fully functioning barbeque set up in between the two courts. A couple of people are handing out burgers and buns. Vampire Weekend is playing from a wireless speaker in a corner.

Most, if not all, of Year 13 are here. It's a *huge* year group compared to the rest of the school—a lot of the Higgs girls from that year group moved to Truham after there was a big fire at Higgs and a few buildings burned down. Long story.

Harry puts his hands on his hips and grins up at me. "Thoughts?"

Harry Greene, a fairly short guy with very tall hair, is probably the most notorious individual in the entire school, partly due to how many parties he throws and partly due to the fact that he never, ever shuts up.

I raise my eyebrows. "About the fort or about your thighs?"

"Both, mate."

"Both are great," I say, deadpan. "Good job. Keep it up."

Harry steps to one side and lunges. "I knew the skirt was a good decision. I should do this more often."

"Definitely."

Harry used to be a pretty nasty person—just one of the many older boys who gave me shit when I was younger and the only out kid in school. But over the years, thankfully, he's gotten over himself and realized that being homophobic isn't cool. Not that I've forgiven him, though. Nick and I still think he's a massive knob.

Still in a lunging position, he asks, "Did Shannon send you? Have you come to shut down our fun?"

"Technically, yes."

"Are you going to?"

"Obviously not."

Harry nods. "You're gonna go far, mate. You're gonna go far."

Nick is usually very easy to spot in a crowd, but today almost everyone is wearing red. There are a few people who clearly couldn't be bothered, one being my sister, Tori, who's in her black Truham uniform, sitting on the blue asphalt in a corner talking to her friend Rita. But apart from her and a couple of others, everyone blurs into one giant mass of red.

"Nick's over there."

I look back at Harry and he's pointing towards the far left corner, grinning at me. Then he starts walking

towards the corner, humming "We're All in This Together," and I follow him.

"NICK, MATE!" Harry shouts over the crowds of Year 13s, all holding food and red plastic cups and taking photos of each other.

And there he is.

He turns round from a small group of people, a slightly dazed expression on his face as if he's not quite sure whether he's imagining Harry's voice.

I have been going out with Nick Nelson since I was fourteen. He likes rugby and Formula 1, animals (especially dogs), the Marvel universe, the sound felt-tips make on paper, rain, drawing on shoes, Disneyland, and minimalism. He also likes me.

His hair is dark blond and his eyes are brown and he is two inches taller than me, if you care about that sort of thing. I think he's pretty hot, but that might just be my opinion.

When he spots us, he waves enthusiastically, and when we finally reach him, he looks at me and says, "All right?"

Nick's *High School Musical* costume consists of a pair of bright red gym shorts and a red tank top. He's pinned a piece of paper to the front with a very badly drawn wildcat on it. If I'm honest, he's had worse outfits.

"You didn't text me back," I say.

He sips his drink. "I was way too busy getting my head in the game."

Then he holds up a disposable camera and, before I have the chance to smile or make sure I look in any way presentable, takes a photo of me.

A second too late I hold up my hand in front of the camera. "Nick!"

He lets out a loud laugh and starts rewinding the camera before putting it in his pocket. "Another one for the Derp Charlie collection."

"Oh my God."

Harry's already wandered off to talk to another group, so Nick steps a little closer and our hands automatically touch, his tapping mine like we're playing a clapping game. "You sticking round here for a bit? Or are you revising?"

I glance round. "I wasn't really revising. I was watching Mac DeMarco concerts."

"Ah. Of course."

We just sort of stand there for a bit, hands touching, and then Nick brings up a hand to adjust my hair slightly. It hits me suddenly that this is the last day we're going to be at the same school. Six entire years of being in the same place every weekday are over. The two years we've been a couple at school, two years of eating lunch together, sitting in form, hiding in music rooms, IT rooms, PE changing rooms, two years of going home together, walking when it's sunny, getting the bus when it's cold, Nick drawing faces in the window condensation, me falling asleep on his shoulder. It's all over.

Normally we talk about this stuff—stuff that we get sad about or annoyed about or angry about—but Nick's really excited about uni so I don't want to start complaining or make him feel bad. I've done more than enough of that in my life, for God's sake. I just . . . I'm the one getting left behind, which is kind of crap, really.

We look up when we hear a small click and a loud laugh. We turn and Harry is holding Nick's camera up to us gleefully. "So bloody romantic. I can't believe I'm gonna have to find a new couple to cockblock at uni."

Nick snatches the camera back. "Did you literally just pickpocket me?"

Harry winks and laughs at him before wandering away again. Nick shakes his head and rewinds the camera. "God, he's so *irritating*."

"Where'd you get the camera from?"

"I bought it. I thought it'd be good to have some actual physical photos to put on my uni wall instead of just crappy photos on my phone."

I grab it out of his hands and take a picture of him.

"Hey!" He grabs it back, grinning. "I don't want pictures of just *me*. Everyone'll think I'm obsessed with myself."

I smile too. "I'll have that one, then."

Nick puts his arm around me. "Okay, we need at least one picture together where we look fucking *normal*." He holds the camera up in front of us, the lens facing us, and I say, "Let's be honest, we never look normal," and Nick laughs at me while I'm making sure my hair isn't doing something weird, and then we both smile, and he takes the picture.

"When I visit you at uni, I'm expecting that one framed," I say.

"Only if you buy me a frame. I'll have rent to pay."

"God, get a job."

"What? You mean you're not going to buy me things now that you have a job? I can't believe this. Why am I even in this relationship?"

"I don't even know, Nick. Why are you still here? It's been over two years."

Nick just laughs and kisses me quickly on the cheek, then starts to walk backwards away towards the drinks table. "You're nice to look at."

I give him the middle finger.

When we first started going out, we didn't tell people for a while. We didn't really know how people would react to us, so it was safer to just be low-key. There hadn't been an openly gay couple in our school, well, *ever*, as far as we knew, and I'd been bullied a lot when I was outed. So we didn't hold hands. We didn't flirt when other people were around. Sometimes I even felt kind of awkward just *talking* to him in school, just in case someone found out and started bullying me again or, worse, started bullying *Nick* too.

Nowadays, we don't have to be scared here. I hold his hand whenever I want.

NICK

So I might've cried when the final bell went. Just a little bit.

I wasn't as bad as Harry. He was bawling his eyes out and hugging everyone, including some scared-looking Year 7s who just wanted to catch their bus.

Even though it's not like today was the last time I'll ever see my friends, it still feels sad. Never wearing our uniforms again, no more lunchtime rounders on the field, the end of Wednesday period-five biscuit hour in the common room.

No more hanging out with Charlie at school.

I guess there are a few things I'm a bit nervous about. Coming out as bisexual again is probably the main one—I mean, I have to come out to someone every other day anyway, but new uni friends means a new load of people who are probably going to assume I'm straight. Leaving home's gonna be scary too. I'm a bit worried about my mum being by herself all the time.

And, again, there's leaving Charlie behind.

Still, there are loads of good things about leaving school—*God*, I'm ready for university, for doing my own thing whenever I want, for actually learning stuff I'm *interested* in. Finally getting out of this dingy town, having my own place, buying my own food, choosing how to spend my time.

It's scary. And I'll miss a lot of things. But I'm ready to go.

"Harry wants to know whether we'll be at his leavers'

party tomorrow," Charlie says from the passenger seat of my car, scrolling through something on his phone. People we know usually message Charlie these days when they want to talk to either of us because I'm horrific at replying to messages. He's way more organized than me.

"Well, I'm still up for it if you are," I say, turning the car out of the school car park.

"Yeah, we should probably go, since prom's going to be crap."

"Fair."

We sit in comfortable silence as I drive us to my house. Charlie picks up his sunglasses from the door compartment and puts them on, then turns the radio on and continues scrolling through his phone, probably through Tumblr, his knees bent and his feet on the seat. Honestly, it's a beautiful day. Blue skies all round, reflecting off town windows and cars. I roll my window down and turn up the radio, and then I take my disposable camera out of my pocket and quickly take a picture of Charlie, his face all sunlit, his dark hair being blown about by the wind, his body curled up on the passenger seat.

He looks at me instantly, but he's smiling. *"Nick!"*

I grin and look back at the road. "Don't mind me."

"At least give me some warning."

"That's not as fun."

This is normal for us, going to one of our houses after school. We spend more time at my house, generally. As my mum's usually at work and my brother's got his own place now, we have the house to ourselves. Over the past few months, our parents have been letting us stay over at each other's houses sometimes, even on school nights. My mum never minds, but Charlie's parents are stricter and Charlie thinks that if he asked more than a couple of times a week, they'd start saying no.

We get that this isn't, like, *normal* normal. We think

our parents see it's not normal as well. I mean, don't get me wrong, they're fine with it, but . . . normal teenage couples don't sleep round each other's houses on school nights, do they? They don't spend every single day with each other, right? I don't know.

We don't care.

★

Things me and Charlie do together at our houses include:

Play video games. Watch TV and films. Watch YouTube videos. Homework. Coursework. Revision. Nap. Make out. Have sex. Sit in the same room on different laptops in silence. Play board games. Make food. Make drinks. Get drunk. Plan trips to concerts. Plan holidays. Build pillow forts. Have sex in a pillow fort (okay, it was only once, but it did happen, I swear). Play with my dogs, Henry and Nellie. Help Charlie's brother, Oliver, with various Lego projects. Talk. Argue. Shout. Cry. Laugh.

Cuddle. Sleep. Text each other from different rooms. Charlie practices his drums, makes playlists, reads books. I take photos on my phone, draw on Charlie when he's not looking, make meals neither of us has tried before.

We're pretty chill. Maybe kind of boring. But, in all honesty, that's fine with both of us.

Today's nothing different. We get in, we get drinks, I change into some jogging bottoms and a sweatshirt. Charlie changes into some jeans and a T-shirt he left here yesterday, and then collapses onto my bed, stretches out on his stomach, and opens my laptop.

"D'you want any food?" I ask as I'm about to go downstairs.

I always ask him this after school. Charlie had anorexia pretty badly the year we started going out. He had to go to a psychiatric hospital for a couple of months and it really helped, but I guess he still sort of has it. Stuff like that doesn't go away very quickly. But

he's nowhere near as bad as he used to be and he's better in lots of other ways too. He's usually fine with main meals now, even if he doesn't eat snacks, like, ever.

"Nah, I'm good," he says, as usual.

I always make sure to ask, though. I think he might say yes one day, if I just keep asking.

Once I've made my way through two slices of toast and a glass of lemonade, I come back upstairs to find Charlie frowning at the laptop screen.

I fall onto my bed next to him. "What's up?"

He glances at me and then back at the laptop before clicking on something. "Nothing. Just reading something on Tumblr."

I don't have Tumblr, despite Charlie trying to make me use it many times. I don't really think it's my sort of thing.

Charlie rolls onto his back to make room for me and takes out his phone. I lie down next to him and pull the laptop towards me. He's already exited Tumblr, so it probably wasn't anything I would have been interested in.

On another tab is the page I started reading this morning about the University of Leeds rugby team, which I'm gonna try and join when I get there, if I'm good enough.

That's where I'm going in September—the University of Leeds. It's pretty far away; like, two hundred miles or something, and me and Charlie have obviously talked about the fact that we'll be long distance. While it's not ideal and nowhere near as great as the way we hang out every day at the moment, we're both completely fine with it. Charlie has a part-time job at a café now, so he reckons he can get the train to see me every few weeks, and I can get the train back every few weeks, and that means we'll definitely see each other at least every two weeks, if not more. And we'll text and call and FaceTime loads anyway.

I start telling Charlie all the facts about the Leeds rugby team—how many tiers there are at the university and whether I think I'll be able to get in (I honestly do—I mean, I'm pretty good at rugby, in my opinion), how much their gym membership is and whether I'll be able to get a job somewhere when I get there, whether it's worth trying to get a sports scholarship, whether I'll be really crap compared to everyone else, and how nice their uniform is (green and white).

Charlie stays still on his back and listens and asks a few questions, but after I've been rambling on for a while I can tell he's getting bored because his voice quiets and he starts fiddling with my sweatshirt sleeve. Then, as I'm in the middle of a sentence, he rolls onto his side and pulls me down by the back of my neck for a kiss, which sort of takes me by surprise because we're long past the stage of needing to make out every time we're alone.

After a few seconds I go to move backwards, but he just pulls me farther down. I laugh against his lips and I feel him smile too, but neither of us stop and after a minute or so I feel my hand subconsciously reach to run through his hair. This is a bit of an odd time of day for us to be doing this, but it's difficult to care, especially when he surges forward so he's lying on top of me.

"Did you want to talk about something else?" I murmur, wondering where this has come from. I push his hair back from his forehead. I probably have a thing for Charlie's hair.

He meets my eyes. Then he sits up, leans back, and switches on the radio. The Vaccines are playing. He moves back down, tilts his head, and says, "Not really," and then his lips are on mine.

CHARLIE

Basically, I hate hearing Nick talk about university.

I'm a horrible person.

He's ridiculously excited about going to uni. And he should be. I'm glad he is.

But lately he's been talking about it *all of the time*. And every single time he mentions it, it just reminds me that we're approaching the end of this. That come September, I'm getting left behind.

Basically, I'm scared.

People keep messaging me on Tumblr about it too,

and they haven't been helping. I've got quite a lot of followers on Tumblr and many of them are interested in Nick and me. Like, *really* interested. It's a little creepy, actually.

So as soon as I mentioned that we'd be long distance from September, I was *flooded* with Tumblr asks about how I should be prepared for all the horrible things that come with long-distance relationships. And they're pissing me off. I stopped answering them a couple of days ago, but people are still sending them. I don't even understand why all these people care that much to make the effort to send me messages about it.

Thankfully, Nick doesn't mention university for the rest of the day, not when we take his dogs for a walk, not during dinner, not while we're watching *Alien*. When he wanders off to have a shower at around ten o'clock, I check my Tumblr inbox again, and there are even *more* now.

Anonymous said:

Have you talked to Nick about what it's gonna be like when he goes away? I know so many couples that tried to make it work when one of them went to uni and they all ended up breaking up. You should really at least talk to him about it.

Anonymous said:

isn't it weird u've been together so long tho??? like 14 is so young to get into a relationship. u shouldn't feel like u have to stay in ur first relationship forever . . .

Anonymous said:

Dude long distance never works, trust me it's better to end it now and save yourself the pain

Anonymous said:

Everyone should go into uni single!! University years are your sexiest years!! Gotta bang as many people as you can!!!!

I don't really want to bring this up with Nick because I don't want him to feel *bad* for going to university. He's completely right to be excited about it.

It doesn't matter how I feel about it.

Nick returns from the bathroom in just pajama shorts, rubbing a towel over his hair. "What's up?"

"What?"

"You're frowning again."

I quickly close the Tumblr app. "Am I?"

He walks over to the mirror and picks up his hair dryer. "Yep."

"Maybe that's just my face."

"Nah, your face is usually way nicer."

I hurl a pillow in his direction, but he steps to one side to dodge it, laughing.

I can't tell him about this. He'd feel awful. He's had enough of feeling bad because of me. I've already been the most annoying boyfriend in recorded history, what with all my mental health stuff.

"Come take a selfie with me," I say. "I want to piss off my Tumblr followers."

Nick grins and puts down the hair dryer. "Why would that piss them off?"

"Selfies piss everyone off."

"So passive aggressive." He walks over to the bed and flops down next to me.

I open the camera on my phone and before he has the chance to say anything about it, I kiss him on the cheek and take the photo like that.

Nick laughs again. "Oh, you're doing that on the internet now, are you?"

I wrap my arms around him. "You know it's what they all want."

"At least let me sort out my hair."

"It looks good when it's wet."

We lean our heads together and I make a peace sign with one hand and take another picture. Then I take one of us actually kissing, but I don't put that one on Tumblr. Some things are nicer if they're just for us.

NICK

The next morning I wake up to the sound of Charlie's phone alarm—he always sets it to an annoying, unignorable beeping sound rather than music like I do. Despite this, waking up next to Charlie is definitely better than any other way of waking up. I don't really know why. My bed always feels sort of cold when he's not there.

Charlie's still insisting he has to go to school today because he's bad at revising at home, so he's making me get up at seven o'clock in the morning to drive him. While I could go to school to revise, the idea of trying to revise on the first day of my study leave kind of makes me want to burn all my revision notes, and also we're both crap at doing schoolwork when we're together anyway.

I open my eyes to see him stirring. A line of sunshine falls across his chest through the gap in the curtains, and even while I'm still half-asleep I get another sudden urge to take a picture of him. Then I remember that I already took one of him asleep last night anyway, when I found him curled up in my bed after I'd gone to get a glass of water, and that had used up the camera film.

Charlie rolls over to turn off the alarm and then goes to climb over me to get out of bed—my bed's situated against the wall—but as he does I slide my hands round his waist and pull him down on top of me. He lets out a surprised noise and then a small laugh, his voice still sleepy. "I have to go shower—"

"No, stay here."

"I can't. I'll fall asleep again."

"Don't go to school."

"Nick!"

"Stay here with me."

"I can't—I've got to . . . I need to revise."

"Mm, fine." I loosen my arms so Charlie can wrestle himself out of them. As soon as he's gone, my bed feels cold and empty again. It's pretty dumb, really. I sleep alone most of the time.

two

CHARLIE

I sort of hoped Nick might have picked up on how I've been feeling. Normally he's pretty good at that—like, *weirdly* good, actually. And I'm not exactly subtle in my attempts to get him to stop talking about uni. But by third period, after I text Nick to see whether he's awake again (after dropping me off at school, he said he was going back to bed), the excited text onslaught begins.

Nick Nelson

(11:34) *We should go uni shopping soon!!! Is it weird I'm excited about buying kitchen utensils?*

Nick Nelson

(12:02) *Dyou think I should email to check whether I'll have a double bed?? Like how do people know which sheets to buy?*

(12:05) *I'd better have a double bed lol your bed is bad enough*

Nick Nelson

(12:46) *Dyou think I should take my xbox or is that too unsociable? I need people to like me*

Nick Nelson

(12:54) *Is Kaleem in school?? If he is can you ask him whether he knows about the beds?*

Nick Nelson

(13:15) *I'm way more interested in home furnishing than I thought. The ikea website is a dangerous vortex*

I reply to all his messages and really try to be enthusiastic, but I can tell my texts sound a bit flat. Nick doesn't seem to notice, though. He just keeps texting me about university and buying stuff for his room and the modules he thinks he wants to take and all sorts of other things that just make me feel increasingly awful by the second.

We've talked about it before. Quite a while ago actually, back when Nick was looking round universities last summer and when he was applying to them in the autumn. I admitted I was pretty worried about him leaving. I said I was scared of being on my own all the time. It was kind of embarrassing, really. Stupid. *Scared of being on my own.* I sounded like I was three years old.

Nick obviously reassured me we'd talk all the time anyway and everything would be fine. We haven't talked about it much since then, but only because there's not much more to say about it.

Everything is going to be fine.

I sit in the common room and listen to Muse's *Origin of Symmetry* album on repeat and focus on my classics revision, trying to memorize some Latin vocab, getting Aled, my only friend in school today, to test me every now and then. I just need to stop thinking about it all. Everything's fine. I'm worrying about nothing.

After lunch, after I've failed for the third time to remember what *latrocinium* means, Aled puts down my pack of cue cards and looks at me. Aled Last doesn't have a load of friends—he's extremely shy so not many people try to talk to him—but I'd say he and Tao are two of my best.

"Ugh, sorry," I say immediately. "Wow. I need to revise more. God."

Aled blinks at me, and then glances out the window. It's another intensely sunny day. I probably should have just stayed in bed with Nick this morning.

"Maybe we should stop revising now," he says in his tiny voice. He chuckles and looks down at his own revision—more colorful maths cue cards. "Not that I've been doing much anyway."

"Haha, yeah, same."

"You okay, though?" he asks. "I feel like you've been really down today."

I pause, a little taken aback. "Oh. Yeah. No. I'm fine."

"Yeah?" He fiddles with his fingers and gives me a look.

"Yeah. I don't know. Nick's just talking a lot about uni, it's kind of . . . just makes me feel a bit crap . . . I don't know." I groan and run a hand through my hair. "That sounds so bad when I say it out loud."

"No, you're allowed to feel things." He smiles. "I get it."

"It's not really fair on him, though. Like, he has a right to be excited."

"Maybe you should talk to him about it. You've already talked about long distance and stuff, right?"

"Yeah, we've talked about it . . . I just don't think he realizes how much it's . . ." I don't really know how to finish my sentence. "It'll make him feel so bad, though." I shake my head. "I don't want him to stop being excited about it."

"Well . . ." Aled struggles to find something to say. He looks down at his desk and fiddles with his cue cards. "I don't think you've got anything to be worried about. I mean, you know, you're . . . you're Nick and Charlie. You're not going to break up . . . I don't think . . . I mean, even Elle and Tao aren't breaking up and you know what they're like."

Tao's been going out with Elle Argent, a girl from Nick's year, for almost the same amount of time Nick and I have been going out. They do seem to bicker a lot, but it's usually about very trivial things such as opinions about movies.

"Yeah."

Aled doesn't say anything else, so I stand up and say I'm going to the bathroom. But I don't go to the bathroom. I walk all the way down to the locker room, just so I can lean against a wall in a locker row and take out my phone and try and think of something to say to Nick, some way of telling him what I'm feeling. But there isn't any way to say it, not without making him feel guilty. And that's the last thing I want.

Instead, I load up my Tumblr inbox, just to see if there's anything interesting in there, but there are only a few new messages asking whether I've thought properly about how long distance works, about whether it's really worth the pain, about whether Nick's really not going to meet anyone else at university while I'm not with him all the time. I don't mean to let this stuff get to me, but it still does. I even feel myself start to well up a bit, so I exit the Tumblr app and delete it from my phone.

We're fine. Why am I getting upset about this now?

NICK

When Charlie slumps into my car at 3:15 p.m., I can tell something's up. I say hi but all I get is a tiny grumble in response, and as soon as he shuts the door he leans on the window and closes his eyes.

I stay still for a moment, waiting to see if he's going to say anything. But he doesn't. "You okay?"

"Mm," he says, unmoving.

"Bad day?"

"Mm."

I drive off without pushing it. If he wants to talk

about it, he will. That's one thing I've learned about Charlie: If you try and make him talk about stuff he doesn't want to talk about, there's even less of a chance he'll eventually tell you.

By the time we get to Charlie's house he seems a bit better, so I don't bring it up. But something's still kind of *off* with him. He sits at his laptop in intense silence while I'm catching up with his mum. He spends at least half an hour choosing what to wear for Harry's party, even though he wears the same jeans and checked shirts everywhere anyway. It takes him significantly longer than normal to eat dinner, which is always a sign he's stressed about something. In the car on the way to Harry's house, his knees bob up and down.

Maybe he's pissed off at me for some reason. I have no idea why he would be.

We park down the road and he walks a little way ahead of me and Tori, who we gave a lift to.

"Have you argued?" Tori asks. "Seems like he's pissed off with you."

"Not that I know of. I don't know what's wrong."

"Hm." She doesn't say anything else.

Harry Greene lives in a town house near the high street. His massive parties are pretty much the main reason he's the most famous guy at Truham. We know that by eleven almost everyone will be in the basement dancing to some crappy dubstep remixes. By twelve, people will be throwing up in house-plant pots and on the sidewalk outside. By two, people will be asleep in corridors, breaking away into different rooms to mess around, and getting high in the garden.

Sure enough, Harry's got music blasting from the basement, making the floor vibrate, and there are people everywhere, mostly Truham sixth formers, but definitely a few Year 10s and 11s too, and people from the secondary school across town. I think we were all supposed to be in the garden, but it's started chucking it down with rain. So much for summer.

As soon as we're inside and Tori's gone off to find her friends, Charlie speed-walks towards the kitchen for drinks. The kitchen table, as expected, is covered in bottles and plastic cups, and once we reach it Charlie downs a vodka shot, and then another one. I think this might be the point where I need to actually say something.

I touch his arm. "Hey."

He looks at me and takes a sip of the vodka-lemonade he just made. "Hm?"

"You okay?"

He nods a little too enthusiastically. "Yeah. Fine. Why?"

I shake my head. "You just seem sort of on edge."

He looks away again and pours a drop more vodka into his drink. "Oh. Just . . . a bit stressed because of revision . . . just been in a bad mood today . . ."

This seems like a reasonable explanation, I guess. Then again, Charlie could lie for Britain—he lies to *loads* of people. He lied to people at school for months about his anorexia. He lies to his parents sometimes when he wants to go out somewhere with me but isn't sure they'd let him. He lies to Mr. Shannon to avoid becoming unpopular with other students. To be fair, he hardly ever lies to me, but occasionally I can tell that he's saying something just because he doesn't want to bother me. I think this might be one of those times.

He takes another sip. His eyes dart around the room. "Best Coast," he says.

"What?"

"The music. It's Best Coast."

I hadn't even clocked that there was music playing in here. I try to think of something to say but he beats me to it.

"We should get drunk."

I chuckle. "I'm driving."

"Oh."

"You get drunk."

"I plan to."

"D'you think we should actually socialize first?"

He pours a glass of lemonade and hands it to me. "Mm, fine." He steps close to me, so close I almost

think he's going to go in for a kiss right here in front of the people chatting and drinking around us, but instead he just gazes up at me beneath dark hair with icy eyes, smirking slightly, the tease of a dimple in one cheek, letting loose everything that made me physically attracted to him in the first place. I'm half confused and half extremely flustered.

"Nick," he says, so low and quiet I probably wouldn't hear it if I weren't staring at his lips.

I let out a nervous laugh, feeling my cheeks getting hot, but don't really know what to say. We're not exactly averse to public displays of affection, but we're never like *this* when other people are around. What is he trying to do?

"I want a drunk hookup in the bathroom later," he murmurs, and then he walks off before I have the chance to answer him.

CHARLIE

I am aware that I am combating my feelings about Nick going to university by a) refusing to talk about it and b) flirting with him so hard it's actually embarrassing, but honestly, I'm *this close* to punching the next person who even uses the word *university* in a sentence. I have not punched anyone yet in my life, but it's never too late to start.

Oh, and c) I am getting drunk.

Very drunk.

It doesn't take a lot to get me drunk, which is

extremely useful for situations like this, where Year 13s are everywhere and no one will shut up about leaving school and prom and summer and university and I just want to go *home*.

I stay away from Nick as much as possible because hearing him talk about it is the worst part of all of it.

I am a terrible person.

It's eleven o'clock now and I've lost count of how many vodka-lemonades I've had, and I'm having to stay seated on an armchair next to Tao in the conservatory because standing up is proving quite difficult at the moment. There isn't really enough room for both of us on the armchair and my leg is sort of going numb because Tao is slightly sitting on it, but he's too engrossed in talking about something or other, I don't know, I'm not really paying attention—

"Have you and Nick talked about it?" he says, snapping me out of my daze. But it's still like I've got cotton wool in my ears and nothing that's happening is actually happening.

"What? I wasn't listening."

Tao grins at me. He always seems more like his eccentric self when we're outside of school. Tonight he's wearing a stripy shirt that was probably intended for a businessman, with rolled-up green trousers and his signature red beanie. He genuinely does think he belongs in a Wes Anderson film.

He throws his arms around me and rests his head on mine. "Aw, you're such an adorable lightweight. I'm glad we're not leaving school this year."

"If one more person mentions leaving school, I'm literally going to cry."

He pats my cheek. "There, there. It'll all be fine. You're Nick and Charlie, aren't you?"

"I don't know what that means," I say.

NICK

Everyone is talking about uni.

I don't think I've ever been so excited for something, or so *ready*. And everyone else going to uni seems to agree. It's the start of freedom. Doing things because we *choose* to do them. Finally being treated as *adults*.

But I get that, like, Charlie might not want to talk about it all the time. I mean, he's still got a year of school left.

It gets to eleven and Charlie is definitely avoiding me. Normally we stick pretty close together at parties, and considering how he was acting earlier . . . well, I'm a bit confused, if I'm honest.

I find him curled up in an armchair with Tao. I say hi to Tao and exchange pleasantries but can see Charlie staring at me. I crouch down next to the armchair so our eyes are level. His are unfocused and he's blinking a lot—he's drunk, all right. "You okay?"

"I'm *fine*," he snaps, with an irritated grin. "God, you don't need to, like, check up on me every second, Jesus Christ."

I feel myself recoil. Charlie hasn't snapped at me like that for *months*. What the hell have I done?

I stand up again. "All right. Fine. No need to shout at me."

He looks away. "I wasn't shouting."

"Yeah." I turn around and go to leave the conservatory, but not so fast to avoid hearing Tao say to Charlie, "What's going on?"

CHARLIE

It's midnight and I'm in the basement, where almost everyone's come to dance, hoping that the blast of dubstep, some crappy remix of a Daft Punk song, will drown out the buzzing in my brain, but it doesn't. I can't stop thinking I'm a piece of shit, I'm the worst boyfriend in the entire universe. I lean against the wall but just end up sliding down it so I'm sitting on the floor, all the dancers blurring in front of me under Harry's flashing fairy lights. Why am I being so weird and angry? Why am I like this?

"Charlie!" shouts a voice over the music, not Nick's, and I look up and there's Aled, gazing down awkwardly in his burgundy jumper. He squats down next to me. "Are you all right?"

I swallow, so close to saying no. No, I'm ridiculous, I'm hilariously un-all-right. "Yeah, yeah, I'm fine."

"You don't look all right." Aled frowns. "Did you . . . is this because of Elle and Tao?"

Maybe I'm just hallucinating conversations now, maybe my brain is just stringing random words together. "What? What d'you mean?"

"I just thought . . . you know . . . what I said about Elle and Tao yesterday . . . like . . . it was stupid, I feel really bad . . ."

I shake my head, wanting to laugh. "What the fuck are you talking about, Aled?"

"You know . . . Elle and Tao breaking up."

I spring forward from the wall. *"What?"*

Aled's eyes widen. "Oh, oh, God, I assumed you would know by now. They just decided that they're breaking up at the end of summer, I heard . . ."

I stare at him.

"What?"

Aled looks down. "Yeah . . . Tao was just like, *Yeah, we're gonna keep on going out until Elle leaves but we think long distance will be too hard."*

"But, Tao didn't tell me . . . I was talking to him earlier . . . I don't . . ."

Aled says nothing.

I open my mouth to say something else, but nothing comes out. Why would anyone just end a relationship because it's got to go long distance for a bit? Elle and Tao clearly like each other a lot. They pined over each other for *ages* before they started dating.

Why would anyone do that?

Nick and I aren't going to do that. Nick thinks long

distance will be fine. He doesn't want to break up with me.

Does he?

Does he want to break up with me?

"Oh God, Charlie, what's . . ." Aled's started speaking because I've started crying. Great.

"Sorry . . ." I say, but my voice definitely isn't audible above the deafening music and I'm not sure who I'm apologizing to anyway. "Sorry . . . I'm so sorry . . ."

NICK

Since I haven't seen Charlie for half an hour, I think now might be a good time to go looking for him again, even if he is in a mood with me. What is his *deal*, though? He's actually starting to piss me off a bit now. I've done nothing for him to be in a mood with me about.

I find him in the basement and he's just sitting in a corner with his friend Aled, so I go over to him, hoping that his weird bad mood has gone away. But as I barge through the dancers, getting closer and closer, I start to realize that his cheeks are damp and he's been *crying*, and that's when I start to feel seriously concerned. Something's definitely wrong.

I kneel down next to him, and Aled gives me this panicked look like he doesn't know what to do. Charlie rolls his head towards me and he's even drunker than earlier, if that's possible. No wonder he's sitting on the floor in the basement.

"What's wrong?" I shout over the music.

He laughs but it looks wrong, something is really wrong. "Are you gonna start talking about university again?"

"What?"

"It's pissing me off so much, Nick."

I squint at him and ask, "Pissing you off?" but he just mumbles something in reply and I can't hear him properly.

Then he pulls me towards him with one arm and kisses me.

I quickly discover drunk kisses are not fun when one person is sober—I can feel the dampness of his cheeks and he tastes of alcohol. It takes a few seconds for me to actually realize what's happening and in that time, I blink and see Aled make a look of startled distress, stand up, and walk away.

I gently push Charlie off me. "No. You're drunk."

"Niiiick." Charlie tries to lean forward again but I just lean backwards.

"Charlie, you're acting really weird."

"No, I'm not."

"Yes, you are." I pull him by the arm so we're both standing. He staggers and grabs on to my arm with both hands. "Come on, let's go upstairs."

He doesn't answer, so I lead him back through the dancers and back upstairs, where it's nearly empty now—almost everyone is dancing in the basement. I guide him to the conservatory, which is, as I'd hoped, empty and quiet, apart from the rain that's pummeling against the glass roof.

I sit him down on the armchair again and crouch in front of him. "What's going on?"

He doesn't look at me, or even seem to have heard me.

"Char." I say this a little louder and this time he meets my eyes. "Why are you acting like this?"

"What?" he snaps, shaking his head. "What am I *acting like*?"

"Like one minute you're seriously pissed off with me and the next you want to get off with me!"

He bends over and puts his head in his hands. "I feel sick."

"For fuck's sake." I stand up. This is hopeless. "Why are you being such a *dick*?"

He doesn't move.

"Just talk to me!" I say.

71

He says nothing.

"You can't be angry at me if you can't even tell me what I'm doing wrong!"

He makes a groaning noise and shakes his head in his hands.

"Fucking *hell*," I say, sitting down heavily on the sofa opposite. "Well, I don't fucking know what to do, then."

"Stop shouting at me," he mumbles from behind his hands.

"I'm not shouting at you!"

"You *are*."

We sit in silence for a minute until a particularly loud thunder crash makes me jump. Charlie notices and raises his head.

"You can break up with me if you want," he says.

It takes a few seconds to process that.

"What?" I say. I stand up again and feel myself *really* getting angry now. What is he *talking* about? Where the hell has this *come from*? "What the *fuck* are you talking about?"

"If you ... want a fresh start, or ... something ... if you think long distance is too hard ..." His eyes are unfocused again, his words slurring. Lightning flashes overhead, brightening the room. Why is he saying these things?

"What? Is that what *you* want?" I huff out a laugh. This can't be happening. "You want us to break up. Is that it?"

"I just ... want you to be ... happy ..."

"Bullshit," I spit out, my voice definitely too loud now.

"Elle and Tao are breaking up ..."

"What, so we need to break up too? You're not even going to *try* to stay in a relationship with me?" Part of me wants to talk this out rationally, but most of me is just pure *anger*, and I don't even know why. I think I'm just tired of all this. Tired of all this bullshit and all this university talk and remembering that I've only got a few months left with Charlie.

"Why are you saying these things, Charlie? If you're trying to break up with me, just fucking spit it out."

But I don't want him to. I feel like I'm about to be sick.

Charlie just shakes his head and stares blankly at the space next to me.

"Is that why you've been acting like this?" I say. "You want to break up with me, but you're not even fucking brave enough to say it? You want to force me to break up with you instead?"

He's crying again now, his head shaking from side to side and his knees bobbing up and down. But he doesn't say anything. He doesn't deny it.

"Well, fuck you, then," I say, and that's when I realize that I'm crying too. God, how long's it been since that happened?

And then he ⸱

me. "Well, it's *me* w

towards somewhere ⸱

voice breaks. "You're fu⸱

you'll meet loads of new peo⸱

left behind. We keep being like,

be fine, we'll FaceTime loads, blah ⸱

going to be all right, is it?" He gestu⸱

darting around the room. "It's *not* going

it's going to be *crap* for me. I'm going to be

shitty town all by myself, but here you are, talk⸱

it like it's the fucking *best thing ever,* and you know

It makes me feel like *shit.* It's like you're looking forw⸱

to getting rid of me, like you can't *wait* to finally ge⸱

out of here and get away from me—"

"What the *fuck*?!" I shout back, running a hand

through my hair. "What d'you want me to do?! *Not* go

to university?"

"No!"

"Becaus⸱

"I'm n⸱

"You'⸱

about

unive⸱

H⸱

the⸱

e that sounds like what you're saying."

ot—"

ve got no *fucking right* to be annoyed with me

hat. I'm a year older than you, I'm going to

rsity in September. That's just the way it is."

e stares at me, eyes wide and filled with tears, and

n he looks down. "Why are you being like this?"

"Mate, what the fuck am I *being* like?"

Charlie looks up again, and when he moves his hand,

his eyes are thin slits.

"Don't call me *mate*. You never call me *mate*."

I just shake my head and let out a huff of exasperation.

"You really are being a proper dickhead tonight,

aren't you?"

"Just leave, then!" he shouts. The rain falls harder than

ever—I can barely hear him over the noise. "Fuck off,

then!"

"Yeah, fine. No problem."

And that's it. I walk out of the room.

Standing in the corridor is Tao, who has probably heard every word. God, this is all his and Elle's fault. If they hadn't fucking broken up in the first place, Charlie wouldn't . . . he wouldn't want to . . . he wouldn't have thought he'd . . .

"Is he . . . Are you okay?" Tao stutters.

"See what you've done?" I say, stepping past him. "Fuck you." He cowers back. I want to say something else to him, but I can't think of anything, my mind's gone blank, I'm still processing what's just happened. What *has* happened? Everything was fine yesterday. This can't be the end. This can't possibly be the end.

I barge through the people chatting and smiling and laughing in the living room until I'm out of the house and in the rain, and by the time I reach my car I'm soaked and shivering. I turn the engine on but I just end up sitting in my car for twenty minutes, maybe because I'm too scared to drive when I can still hear thunder in the distance, or maybe because I'm hoping Charlie's going to run out of the house and open the door and say that everything he'd said was a drunken mistake. But he doesn't. So I just sit there.

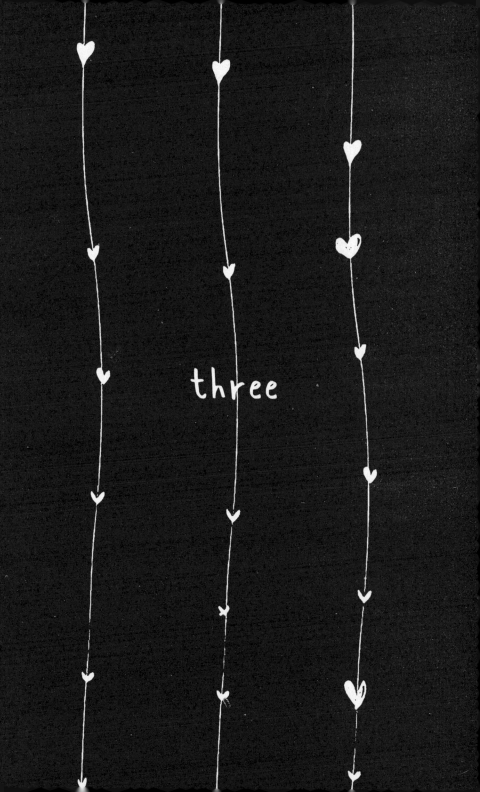

three

CHARLIE

I wake up because the sun is in my eyes—I forgot to close my curtains last night. I forgot to do a lot of things last night. Like be a decent human being.

I fumble for my phone before realizing it's still in my back pocket, and I'm still in my clothes. It's quarter past ten in the morning. No texts, no Facebook messages, nothing. I don't want to get out of bed to change. I don't want to do anything.

I don't want to do anything.

Last night . . .

What was I even *thinking*?

The Elle and Tao thing freaked me out. That after all this time, they'd just be, like, "Cool. Yeah. We're breaking up. Oh well."

After *two years*. Don't they . . . don't they *love each other*?

No. I guess not.

And I guess I started to think, *What if Nick's bored?*

We don't do many exciting things. We just sit around at each other's houses.

I'm pretty boring as a person.

So I guess I wanted to test him, to check whether he wanted to break up, but I couldn't even *say* it. I couldn't even say it properly.

Stupid.

I'm stupid.

I'm a fucking stupid idiot.

I'd rather not have known. I'd rather have just carried

on in blissful ignorance of what he thought, rather than this absolute mess. Now I have no idea what he's thinking. Is he just angry at me, or does he actually want to break up?

The thought of texting him to find out makes me feel physically ill.

We've argued before, but nothing quite as bad as this. We've never woken up still angry at each other. I haven't woken up feeling this shit in a long time, hungover and wanting to be sick and wanting to cry and experiencing that familiar emptiness I thought I'd gotten rid of a long time ago. That feeling that makes me want to stay in bed and never get up again.

One time when I was in Year 11, a few weeks after I got out of the hospital, Nick said something he didn't mean while we were eating dinner—some stupid thing about how I wasn't trying hard enough—and I started having a go at him and it turned into a massive argument, ending with him leaving. But even then, he still came back a while later. And everything was okay again.

I roll over so I'm out of the sun and pull my covers over my head, but the birds tweeting outside are too loud and it's still too bright in my room, so I just end up lying there. I wish I could turn back time. I wish I could keep turning back time to Thursday, and every time I got to the end of Thursday, I'd rewind time to the beginning of Thursday again, and I'd just be with Nick every day for the rest of my life.

Can't believe I even think stuff like this. Pathetic. I'm so pathetic.

"Morning," Tori says when I slump down next to her on the lounge sofa. She's in her pajamas and dressing gown and is watching *Bridesmaids* with a large bag of Kettle Chips on her lap.

"Morning. Why are you watching a film at eleven o'clock in the morning?"

"Why not?"

"Why Kettle Chips?"

"First day of study leave treat."

"It's your second day of study leave."

"Then . . . it's my second day of study leave treat."

I laugh and watch the film with her for a few minutes. I never really got into this film, but Tori's weirdly obsessed with it. It might be because the main character is super sarcastic, just like her.

"So . . . you feeling okay?" She turns to me. "Have you had breakfast?"

"Feel a bit sick. It's nearly lunchtime anyway."

"Hm." She doesn't comment. Normally Tori's the first one to make me eat when I don't want to. "What happened to Nick last night? You're lucky Becky had her car. And why were you drunk and crying in the conservatory?"

I groan and roll my head back against the sofa. "Do we have to talk about it?"

She shrugs and looks back at the screen. "Nope. Thought you might want to."

We sit in silence for a minute.

And then I decide to tell her.

I tell her the full story, not that there's much to tell anyway. Nick constantly talking about university, me getting all anxious about it, hearing about Elle and Tao, getting scared, saying stuff I shouldn't have, Nick freaking out—everything is my fault, as usual.

"Jesus," she says once I've finished. She gazes at me, the remains of her eyeliner smeared under her eyes, and then she pauses the film. "Sounds like a really bad argument."

"Yeah, no shit."

"You don't think he wants to break up, do you?"

"Well, I don't know. Maybe. He didn't say, *No,*

I don't want to break up, you know? He just . . . got so angry . . ." And then suddenly I feel tears in my eyes. I bring up a hand to cover my face and when I speak, my voice is all high-pitched and wobbly. "I feel like shit."

"Oh, Charlie." Tori puts down her crisps and pulls me into a hug, running one hand over my back. "It's okay."

I shake my head into her shoulder, trying not to get tears all over her dressing gown. "It's not okay . . . it's really not okay . . ."

She lets me cry into her shoulder for a few minutes before she speaks again.

"I think you need to talk to him."

"I don't know what to say," I whisper.

"Just something. Anything."

"He hates me."

"That's untrue."

"He's angry."

"That's temporary."

"I don't know what to *say*."

"It doesn't matter what you say," she says. "You just have to say something."

NICK

Saturday is a nothing day. I get up at around ten. I take Henry and Nellie for a walk. I eat. I have a nap. I play with Henry in the living room. I play video games for five hours. I eat again. I nap again. I go on YouTube for four hours. I discover that I've lost my disposable camera. I spend an hour looking for it. And then I cry myself to sleep.

On Sunday morning I stay in bed. I start to realize that the reason I feel numb is because I'm in shock. In shock that Charlie would even suggest breaking up. I also start to realize that the shock is turning into panic, I'm panicking now, panicking that long distance really isn't going to work after all, that it's going to be too hard. If Charlie's this upset now, he'll be even worse when I leave. But I can't stay here just because he's upset about it. What am I supposed to do? There's nothing I can do. Nothing. It is what it is. Charlie wants to break up with me before it gets too painful. Maybe we'd end up breaking up anyway. Maybe we're just getting it out of the way.

What? I don't know. I have no idea what I think anymore.

I go to text Charlie but then realize I can't because I don't know what to say. I can't speak to him until I actually understand what I feel.

I start crying again.

Mum asks me what's wrong on Sunday afternoon.

I tell her me and Charlie had an argument.

"Oh, you two'll get that patched up, though, won't you, love?" she says, and then leaves the kitchen before I have the chance to say: *Not necessarily. Maybe not. Maybe this is it.*

CHARLIE

Wednesday arrives and I still haven't done anything and neither has Nick. I guess I hoped if I waited long enough, he'd be the one to text me first, or call me, or *something*. But there's nothing.

Honestly, I have no idea what he's thinking. Maybe he really *does* want to break up. Why else would he have just lost it at me? He's never been so angry with me before. God, I wouldn't blame him if he wanted to break up. I'm pathetic.

I try to distract myself with revision, but it doesn't

really work. My Thursday Latin language exam rolls around and it goes fine. I memorized all the vocab in the end; there's nothing I'll let stop me from doing my best in my exams. But I don't feel happy when it's over. I just check my phone for the six-hundred-billionth time. And there's nothing, of course. Nothing.

I know I should text him, but if I ask whether he really does want to break up and he says yes, I don't know what I'll do.

What's the point of a life without Nick?

Wow. I'm so embarrassing.

If he wants to talk to me, he will. If he doesn't, then I guess that's it.

That's the end.

NICK

Nine days since the party. A Sunday. I messed up my psychology exam on Friday, but I don't think that was because of our argument. Everyone knows psychology A level came straight out of hell.

I've got a few days until my next exam, so I don't do anything again this weekend. I don't even take the dogs for a walk; I ask Mum to do it. I just sit in my room, curtains shut, playing video games, watching TV, doing nothing.

Mum walks in at around one p.m. to ask if I want

lunch, but stops when she sees me wrapped up like a burrito in my duvet, my hair greasy and a property show on the TV.

She sits down on the bed. "You all right, Nicky?"

"Mmm."

"How's Charlie? I haven't seen him for ages."

I blink slowly and look at her.

"We argued."

"That was a while back, though, wasn't it, love?"

"Nine days."

"And you still haven't sorted it out?"

"No."

"Oh, baby." She pats what she thinks is my leg but is actually just a bit of lumpy duvet. "Have you tried talking to him?"

"He broke up with me."

"What? Are you sure? That doesn't sound like him."

"Yes."

She breathes out. "Oh, baby. I'm so sorry." She holds out her arms for a hug and I sort of fall into them, still in my duvet-burrito form. "It'll be okay. You'll be all right."

It takes quite a lot of effort not to start crying again.

"D'you want to order pizza tonight?" she asks. "Special treat."

I nod. "Yes, please."

"I love you so much, baby. You'll be okay."

"Love you, Mum."

But I don't think I'll be okay. Ever. I don't think I'll ever be okay ever again.

four

CHARLIE

Two weeks after the argument is my penultimate exam—music. A Friday. I don't think about anything except my exams for the entire week. Well, except the fact that I can't remember the last time I spent two *days* away from Nick, let alone two entire weeks. God.

Do I need to start trying to get over this? Because I have no idea how people do that. Nick is the best and most important person I have ever met.

God.

I go out with my friends that evening, just to Simply

Italian for a big end-of-exams celebration meal, even though my last exam isn't until next Thursday. I try to have fun and laugh at people's jokes and talk about how horrible exams were, but everything's fake. I don't want to laugh at anything. I want to go home and sit in bed and do nothing.

Tao's on my left. He's laughing and joking with the rest of our friends, but I can tell he's joining in to hide how sad he is about Elle. How did they decide to break up? Did they just agree it'd be for the best? Or did they have a big argument like me and Nick? I don't want to bring it up and upset Tao more.

On my right is Aled. He stays quiet for most of the evening, as he often does, but as we're all sorting out who's paying what, he says, "Charlie," and I look at him, and I see genuine concern in his eyes.

"Have you spoken to Nick at all?" he asks.

Word of our argument has spread everywhere, obviously.

"No," I say, trying to keep any and all emotion out of my voice.

"So . . . is that it, then?" His voice is almost a whisper. "Have you, erm, broken up?"

"Yeah." I realize that this is the first time I've said it. I've been distracting myself up until this point, but now I don't have revision to distract me anymore. And there it is. We've broken up. "Yeah, I, erm . . . I think so."

Aled looks at me for a long moment. "I'm so sorry."

"Not your fault."

"No, but"—he shakes his head—"you're Nick and Charlie."

I laugh. "What does that *mean*?"

"It's . . ." He laughs too, a nervous expulsion of air. "You're . . . it's hard to explain. It's like, if you had to provide evidence for soul mates, everyone would pick you two."

I snort. "There's no such thing as soul mates."

"Maybe. But you two present a pretty convincing argument."

"If we were, he wouldn't have broken up with me."

"Is that actually what happened?"

I stare at Aled. I've never heard him so assertive. I don't know how to answer.

"Did he actually say, *Charlie, I want to break up with you?*"

I frown. "Well, no, not exactly. But, he didn't say, *I don't want to break up.*"

"But obviously he wouldn't have said that."

"What?"

"If he thought you were trying to break up with him, he's not going to start protesting against it. If he thought you didn't love him anymore, he wouldn't make it difficult for you. He'd just be heartbroken."

"Well, he's an idiot, then!"

Aled laughs. "Exactly. Two idiots in love. Couple goals."

"Great. Thanks."

Someone interrupts us to see whether Aled's sorted out what money he owes. I really want to believe what he's saying. That Nick never wanted to break up.

Maybe it's time to find out.

As soon as I get home, I sit down at the breakfast bar where Tori is sitting with her laptop and a large glass of diet lemonade. She turns to me.

"You look at least two hundred percent more cheerful than you have been collectively in the past two weeks," she says.

"I need to talk to Nick, like, *soon*."

She throws her hands into the air. "Jesus Christ! Finally! Revelation of the century!"

I swivel on the stool. "But also, I really don't want to."

"Yeah, yeah, yeah. You've had your tantrum time, okay? You're a Year 13 now."

"Not till September."

"I always count it from the last day of the year before."

"Well, I don't."

She takes a long sip of lemonade and then points violently at the door. "Go talk to him, you giant child!"

"Oh my God, *fine!*"

I get up from the breakfast bar and wander towards the door, but Tori speaks just as I'm about to leave.

"By the way, I found this stuffed between the sofa cushions." She picks up something next to her and holds out Nick's disposable camera. "Is it yours?"

I take it from her. "Oh, that's Nick's."

"Oh. He might want it back, then."

"Yeah." I walk slowly out of the room. The number on the tiny screen at the back is at zero—I didn't even know Nick had taken that many pictures. When did he take them all? He could only have left the camera here two weeks ago while we were getting ready for the party, and I didn't see him take any then. So it must have been the day before that.

And that's when I know exactly what I'm going to do.

*

Straight after my shift at the café on Saturday morning, I speed-walk to Boots to get the film developed.

I have absolutely no idea what's on it, but I figure there might be something I can send Nick. I don't know whether that'll help anything. But a picture speaks a thousand words, I guess. Blah blah blah, something cheesy and romantic. Yep. Cool.

I arrive at Boots and it turns out I have to wait an hour for them to develop the photos, so I wander around town with my umbrella over my head. I buy an Oreo Dairy Milk bar from a newsagent's because Nick's obsessed with them. Then I sit down on a bench and take out my phone, balancing my umbrella on my shoulder.

And then I see I have a text from Tao.

I open it immediately.

Tao Xu

(15:34) *Hey Charlie, I know the past few weeks have been kind of awful for both of us because of stuff with Elle and Nick but I wanted you to be the first to know that me and Elle are getting back together. We talked about it some more and we're both SHIT SCARED about being long distance . . . but deciding to break up was a mistake. We both still love each other so much haha. So we want to at least try to make it work!!*

My heart nearly thumps out of my chest. Tao and Elle made a mistake. They're *getting back together.*

Charlie Spring

(15:52) *omg. i'm so so happy for you, i know you two are good together*

Tao Xu

(15:54) *Also I'm so sorry if me and Elle caused some weird drama between you and Nick and I really hope it's cool between you guys soon, and if this is at all helpful I saw Nick quickly as he was leaving Harry's and he was really upset about it . . . like I'm pretty sure there's no way he wants to actually break up with you.*

I read the message several times before replying.

Charlie Spring

(15:56) *it's definitely not your fault . . . i'll keep you updated. i don't really want to break up either haha*

And that sort of makes me feel a bit better. Just saying it.

I do not want to break up with Nick.

After that, I wander back to Boots to pick up the photos.

I don't look at them until I'm on the bus home.

The first photo is the one Nick took of me when I found him in the box fort on the last day of school. I look sort of bewildered. My eyes are all wide and my mouth half-open, and it's not a *terrible* photo. It's nice because it looks natural, I guess.

The second is the one Harry took when we weren't looking, and it doesn't look half as awkward as I thought it was going to. We're standing on the grass with our hands touching, just sort of looking at each other like we've come to a pause in conversation, the grass at our feet and the trees overhead looking so bright in the sun. It's kind of arty. Harry would probably be very pleased with himself.

The third is the one I took of Nick, and it *is* a terrible photo. I laugh out loud. It's hilarious actually—he's mid-blink. He'll probably throw it in the bin as soon as he sees it.

And the fourth one is the selfie we took together,

Nick's arm around my shoulders and our heads together, both of us smiling, a little lens flare from the sunshine falling across Nick's chest. I look at that one for a while. That Thursday was such a lovely day. I wish the past two weeks had been as lovely as that day.

There are a few after that still at school, several of Nick with his Year 13 friends and even a couple just of the school building itself, as if Nick just wants to remember what it looks like.

And then there's the one of me in Nick's car. Sitting with my legs tucked up on the seat, my sunglasses on, scrolling through my phone. It's nice. I hardly ever see pictures of me like this; they're almost always selfies or posed photos with friends.

The bus jolts suddenly and the photos fall off my lap onto the seat next to me. I slam my hand down on them before they fall on the floor but they've all spread out like playing cards, and one photo catches my eye.

It's me, asleep in Nick's bed. The streetlights outside send a soft orange glow through the thin curtains behind me. My hand is curled next to my face and my hair has gone all messy and pushed to one side. I don't know when he took this one. I think I fell asleep before him, but I honestly can't remember.

Maybe it's kind of a weird picture to take, but I can understand why Nick took it. I'd take a picture of him if he looked like that in my bed. God, that sounds creepy, doesn't it? I don't care.

As I flick through the rest of the photos, I start to realize that they're all sort of like that, all tinged purple and blue and orange, muted colors, a little blurry, like Polaroids at an art-school exhibition.

Me stretched out on his bed on his laptop. Me lying on the lounge floor with my arms around his border collie, Nellie. Me attempting to give his pug, Henry, a piggyback. Me several steps ahead in the field behind his house when we took the dogs for a walk. Me standing at the top of a hill, holding out my arms—I remember him taking that one. Me giving him side-eye as I caught him trying to take a picture of me against the view, the sunlit horizon and the fields and the river. A selfie of us together. A selfie of us with me holding Henry up so he could be in it too. A selfie of us making stupid faces. Back at his house, a blurred close-up of me laughing from when he'd thrust the camera at my face. The light gets darker, bluer, a photo of me curled up on the lounge sofa, the TV screen illuminating the tips of my hair. Me cross-legged on his bed in just my T-shirt and boxers, pointing at the camera, smiling. And then the one of me asleep.

There are so many of just me.

Me.

Nick just took a ton of photos of me.

Nick's not a hugely creative person. He's never been

interested in photography or art or anything like that.

I think he just took them because he wanted to remember what this was like. What our life is like now. Chilling round each other's houses, going on walks, eating together, sleeping together.

It sounds boring but it's so wonderful.

It is. I feel myself tear up just looking at our life together.

I love this. I love us. I love our weird, boring life.

I take my phone out of my pocket and take a picture of our stupid-face selfie in the field. I send it to Nick.

NICK

My mate Sai has come round to stage an intervention. He's going to Cambridge in the autumn so I'm not entirely surprised that he's smart enough to pick up on the fact that I am approximately seventy miles away from okay, but he hasn't said anything useful so far and now we're playing *Mario Kart* and eating Percy Pigs.

After we've been gaming for around half an hour and chatting casually about A-level revision and summer and how utterly shit Harry's party was, Sai finally says, "So what exactly are you both having an argy-bargy about?" He puts the controller down, swivels round on the sofa, and folds his arms. "Because it sounds like nothing, to be honest."

I sigh and pause the game. "Charlie broke up with me, mate."

"Oh, *come on.* Why the *bloody hell* would he do that?"

"I have no idea."

"Are you sure that's what he was trying to do?"

"Honestly, I'm not even sure. He was so drunk. He kept telling me I should break up with him. And I just lost it at him."

Sai adjusts his glasses and runs a hand through his hair. "Sounds like you need to have a chat with him, dude."

"I don't know what to say." I put my controller down and look at him. "Help me."

"Why am I the relationship expert? I've never even been in a relationship."

"You're smart. You're doing English Lit at uni."

"English Lit is utterly useless in the real world, Nicholas. *Utterly useless.* Trust me. Chaucer and John Donne aren't going to help you with this."

This makes me laugh. "I don't even know who they are."

"Exactly."

I lean my head back on the sofa. "I think he . . . just . . . thought it was a good time to end our relationship. Like, teenage relationships never last. It's a bit weird that we've made it this far anyway. And . . . I dunno, I guess he thinks we're kind of boring; like, we hardly do anything interesting. We're the most basic teenage relationship."

"Basic teenage relationship?" Sai splutters. "Have you seen yourselves? You hang around with each other every single day and somehow haven't wanted to kill each other yet. You've started sleeping round each other's houses regularly on *school nights*! You can communicate by just *looking* at each other! Trust me, I've played board games with you two." He shakes his head. "A basic teenage relationship is daring to hold hands outside the school gate and going on cinema-and-Nando's dates on Saturday afternoons."

I stare at him.

"If you want to break up," he says, pointing a finger at me, "go right ahead. If you're bored and want it to be over, fine. But just because you're not going on fucking amazing dates every weekend doesn't mean you're *boring* and definitely doesn't mean you need to break up."

He slaps his hands on his legs and leans back.

"Shit," I say.

When I pick up my phone a couple of hours later, I have a message.

The name on the screen reads **Charlie Spring**.

five

CHARLIE

I send him another picture two hours later. The one of us kissing that I took on my phone.

Two hours after that, I send him a third picture. The selfie we took in school on his last day.

The next morning, an old selfie of us I find on my Tumblr.

Half an hour later, one of our first selfies, back when we started going out.

And I carry on like that until Monday. Picture after picture until I've sent every single selfie of us I have saved on my phone.

The little Read tick appears on all of them until around Sunday afternoon. Then he stops reading them.

And he says nothing. He doesn't reply.

As soon as Tori gets home from her exam on Monday, I tell her all about it.

"He's not replying," I say. It's actually embarrassing how panicked I sound. "What does that mean?"

She stands at the door, not even taking her shoes off.

"You got those photos?" she says.

"In my room."

"Go get them."

"Why?"

"We're posting them through his letterbox."

"Why will that help?"

"Because texts are dumb." She shrugs. "And a gesture is needed."

I laugh. "Who are you?"

"A born-again woman. Willing to put aside my apathy for the sake of romance." She blinks and puts her hand on her heart. "Jesus, I gave myself indigestion saying that out loud."

Tori's friend Becky drives us. Becky keeps looking at me in the rearview mirror. I've never been truly sure whether Becky likes me or not, but right now, I don't think it matters.

It only takes a minute to drive there, but Tori says we have to drive because a quick getaway will be vital to the success of the "gesture." Sitting in the back seat, I flick through the photos again. Should I post all of them through the letterbox? Just a few? Just one?

I make the decision and take a pen out of my pocket.

NICK

I get home from my Monday afternoon exam, dump my bag on the floor in the hallway, and fall onto the living room sofa. It didn't go too badly today. Only two more to go, and then that's it.

Summer. What am I going to do with all that time?

I almost don't want my exams to end now.

Charlie started sending me blank texts on Saturday while Sai was round. I don't really know what they're supposed to mean. My phone's quite old and I dropped it down the stairs a couple of months ago, so I assume it's a glitch. I haven't turned it on since yesterday afternoon. Seeing Charlie's name keep popping up was making my stomach lurch every single time.

"Nicky? Is that you, love?" my mum calls from the kitchen.

"Yeah," I shout.

"You've got post."

I groan and rise from the sofa. I stumble to the kitchen and walk towards the table, where there's a brown envelope with the word *Nick* on it, no address.

It's in Charlie's handwriting.

And my stomach lurches harder than it has done all weekend.

"Oh my God," I say.

"What's up?" Mum brings two mugs of tea over to the table and sits down, looking at me expectantly.

"It's from Charlie."

Mum gapes. We both stare at the envelope for a long moment.

"Well, open it, then!"

And I do.

Inside the envelope is a photograph—the sort you get developed from disposable cameras. And I know immediately that I took this one. I remember the exact moment I decided to take it, walking into my room after getting a glass of water to find Charlie curled up so beautifully in my bed, the orange streetlamp light shining on his skin, and I felt like if I was going to die, this would be what I wanted to see last.

I turn the photo over and there's Charlie's handwriting.

Hey. You take a lot of pictures of me. D'you have a crush on me or something? How embarrassing. If you wanna talk, I'll be at the Truham Primary School Summer Fete tomorrow (Tuesday) at 3 o'clock . . . wow this isn't a rom-com lol. I'm sorry for how sappy this is. Btw I love you. Ok bye xxxx

CHARLIE

I haven't felt this nervous since I had to do my bloody Head Boy campaign speech in front of the entire school.

What if Nick didn't even see the photo? What if it, like, slipped underneath the doormat? Or his mum threw it away by accident? What if he saw the photo, tore it up, and didn't even notice the note on the back?

What if he read it and still doesn't turn up?

I arrive at Truham Primary School's Summer Fete, which takes place every year on their school field,

with Tori and our dad at around two o'clock. We
spend most of the following hour wandering round
with our younger brother, Oliver, who's in Year 4 at
the school. Dad gives him money to do the tombola
and play on the bouncy castle and the coconut shy. Tori
plays against him on the table football they've got set
up in the middle of the field, and I mainly stand there,
repeatedly checking my phone and searching around
for my boyfriend. Ex-boyfriend? No. Not ex. Not yet.

I'm not giving up yet.

At quarter to three I go and wait near the entrance
to the field, just inside the tennis court. It reminds me
too much of the Truham tennis court, the day when all
this started, all these stupid, pointless feelings.

Charlie Spring

(14:54) i'm in the tennis court!! if ur coming

He doesn't text me back. It doesn't even say he's read the message. I feel myself start to sweat a little. Is this it? Am I going to give up after this? Am I going to be able to give up?

What am I going to say to him? Am I just going to beg him not to break up with me?

What if he turns up and says he still wants to break up?

I take a deep breath.

This is it, I guess.

I look up and watch as Nick walks through the tennis-court gate.

Having not seen him for over two weeks, just the sight of him makes me want to run up to him and kiss him and hold him and not let go of him for at least twenty minutes. I clench my fists and stay very still as he walks up to me. God, everything about him is so perfect.

"Hi," I say as he stops and leans against the tennis

court fence in front of me. I try to think of something else to say, but nothing comes to mind except "You are beautiful" and "I love you."

"Hi," he says, with a nervous smile.

There's a pause.

"I got the photo," he says, and then shakes his head. "Well, duh. Here I am."

I huff out a laugh. "Genuinely the most embarrassing thing I have ever done."

"And you call *me* embarrassing."

"That photo was pretty embarrassing, though."

"True. We're actually both pathetic." He grins and I feel a pang of hope.

"You didn't text me back," I say.

Nick blinks and says, "You were just sending me blank texts. I thought it was a glitch or something." He pulls his phone out of his pocket and shows me his messages. There's the one I sent him five minutes ago, and before that there's just blank message after blank message.

Oh.

Right.

"Why, what did they say?" Nick looks at me curiously.

"Oh ... I was, erm ... sending you all the pictures, like, one by one ..." I run a hand through my hair. "That's so awkward. Wow. Sorry."

"Pictures of us, you mean?"

"Haha ... yeah ..."

"I don't think this phone can get picture messages anymore."

I stare at him. "Can't it?"

"Don't think so. You know I dropped it down the stairs a couple of months ago? It's been doing some weird things since then."

I shake my head, amazed. "I knew you'd dropped it but I didn't know about the photo thing."

He shrugs. "Neither did I."

"Oh."

"Can I see them now?"

He's not laughing at me. He's serious. He doesn't think this was stupid.

"Yeah." I take my phone out of my pocket and we scroll through the pictures one by one, laughing at the stupid ones and pausing on the cute ones. Occasionally we get to one that reminds us of an old day out and we stop and talk about it and remember, remember the silly dates we've been on and the terrible ones and the great ones, the repetitive days we spend indoors and outdoors, at school and at home. By the end, we're both sitting on the asphalt with our backs against the fence, the sun shining off the court and the white of our shoes.

We sit in silence for a minute, and then he says, his voice so quiet I only just catch it over the buzz of the crowd behind us, "I don't want to break up with you."

And I could honestly cry right there. I could just cry with relief.

"Me neither," I say. "Sorry if I sounded like I did. I really didn't."

"Same." He chuckles. "I have no idea what we were arguing about."

"Me neither."

"Sorry I shouted at you. And didn't drive you home."

"Sorry I got drunk and made out with you in front of everyone. And cried."

"Sorry I called you a dick."

"Sorry I told you to leave."

"Sorry for talking about uni all the time."

"Sorry for getting pissed off with you talking about uni all the time."

He laughs, an amazing, boyish, Nick laugh. He rolls his head onto my shoulder. "Can we stop now?"

I find his hand and take it in mine. I lean against him

and he still smells like him. Like home. "Yeah."

"I don't want to break up with you, ever," he says.

"Same."

"Maybe that's stupid."

"I don't care," I say.

"Me neither," he says.

He tilts his head up again and kisses me and I haven't felt like this happy for weeks, months, maybe ever, and something is different too, something I can't quite place. He brings a hand up to my cheek and I don't think things have gone back to normal—instead, we've entered an entirely new era, one where we're better, surer, stronger together.

Wow. I really am embarrassing.

"Also, I bought you chocolate," I say, when we break apart after a while. I take the Oreo Dairy Milk bar out of my pocket, hoping it hasn't melted too much in the heat.

"Oh man." He grabs it and tears it open. "That's it. You've sealed the deal now. We're practically married." He pops a chunk into his mouth and then holds it out to me. "Want some?"

I stare at the chocolate and feel that jolt of fear that I always get, but something, for some reason in that moment, makes me say, "Yeah, okay."

NICK

We decide to ditch the fete. Oliver will be fine with
Tori and their dad, and there isn't really much for us
two to do there anyway. We decide the beach is a much
better idea.

It's about an hour's drive to the beach we always go
to, so Charlie connects my phone to the car radio and
plays some Sufjan Stevens, then Shura, then Khalid.
There are closer beaches, but they're always busy and
disgusting, packed with loud teenagers and toddlers
and people fighting for a spot to lay their towel.

Our beach is a lot smaller. It has a thin pier you can walk down with a bench at the end, and a massive arcade just across the road that stays open until ten p.m. There never seems to be many people on the beach itself, apart from a few dog-walkers and elderly folk, and it's no different today. It's just open space and flat blue sea and a beautiful horizon, as if the whole world has been made just for us.

We walk up and down the beach, talking, and we walk up the pier and sit on the bench at the end and talk and kiss, and then we get the blanket I keep in my car and find a spot on the beach to sit down and then lie down and just be silent for a while.

We walk to the fish-and-chip shop we always go to and sit on the brick wall outside and eat and talk, and then we decide taking off our shoes and socks and rolling up our jeans and paddling in the sea is a good idea but quickly learn, once our jeans get wet, that it probably wasn't a very good idea after all.

We take a bunch of photos on Charlie's phone after talking about how he doesn't take enough. We go to the arcade for an hour and play on all our favorites: air hockey, the jungle car game, the skiing game, the basketball game, the coin machines. We get enough tickets for a bouncy ball.

We sit at the end of the pier again and watch the sunset, because that's what you've got to do on days like this. The clouds turn pink and purple, the sky orange, and then everything is dark blue.

On the drive back, Charlie falls asleep in my car. I turn the radio on and thank the universe that my life is like this.

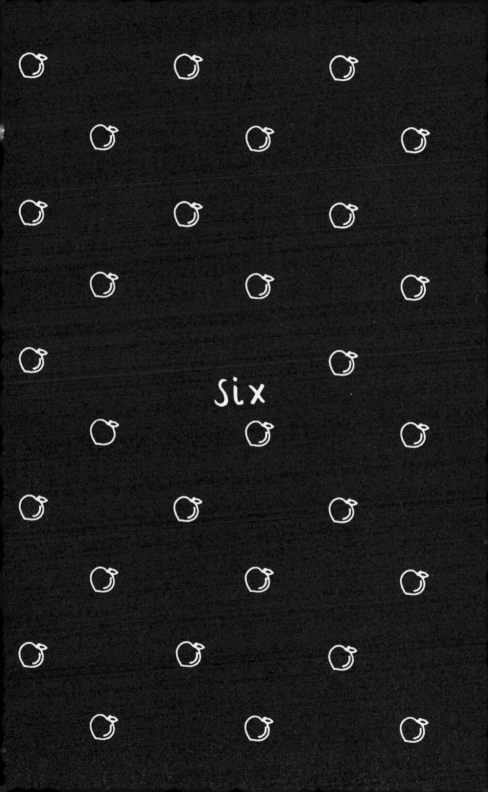

six

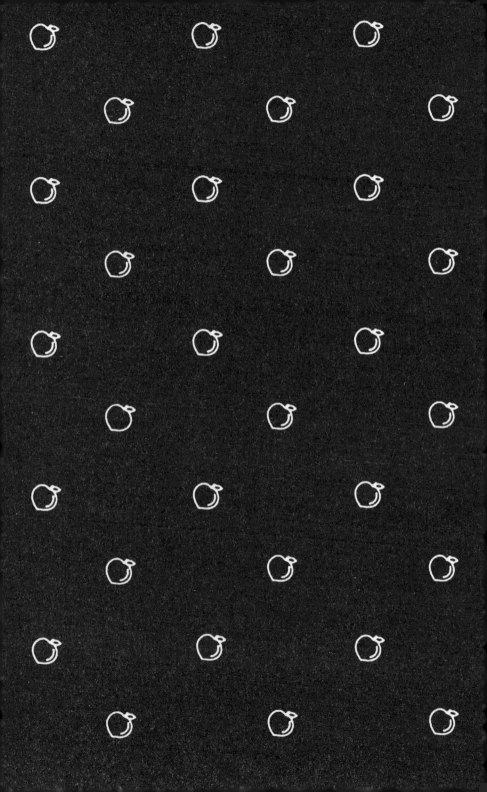

CHARLIE

Aled was right. Nick and I are literally two idiots.

We spend the whole day talking about us and what it's going to be like when we're long distance, and it honestly only makes me believe even harder that we're going to be fine, that everything's going to be okay.

Everything is going to be okay. Seriously, this time.

Nick drives me back home, but I tell him to drive to his house instead. I text Tori that I'm staying over at his. She'll explain to our parents.

We stay up late just talking and browsing the internet and watching videos and talking again, laughing, dozing off. I wonder what it'd be like to have a whole life of this. I think it'd be pretty great. Not gonna lie.

And then one minute we're lying there and the next we're kissing, and it's not like this is anything particularly new, but it *feels* new. It feels like we've been forced apart for a century and this is our reunion, a mix of relief and desperation, both of us clinging to each other on his bed, and when Nick breaks away to kiss my neck I just stop thinking entirely.

How is it that this still makes me so . . . How have two years gone by and I still feel like this in his arms?

We kiss for a long time, like it's two years ago and we're on Nick's lounge sofa trying to watch a film. Impossible. I can't think about anything else when he's running his hands so gently through my hair, across my back, over my hips. I ask if we should take our clothes off and he's saying yes before I've even finished my sentence, and then he's pulling my T-shirt off and laughing when I can't undo his shirt buttons, he's undoing my belt, I'm reaching into his bedside drawer for a condom, we're kissing again, we're rolling over— obviously you can see where this is going.

I don't know if it's because we're feeling especially emotional, or we're just tired, or these past couple of weeks have been too much, but this time reminds me so much of the first time we had sex.

We were both fucking *terrified*, and the whole thing was kind of terrible because we didn't know what we were doing. But it was good too, so good, because we were a mess of emotions and we were scared and excited and everything felt *new*.

So, this sort of feels like that.

Nick touches me like he's scared that any minute

I could disintegrate forever. When we're finally undressed completely he just stops and stares like he's trying to memorize every second of this. When we're moving he keeps saying my name over and over until I find it too ridiculous and tell him to shut up, but he just grins and keeps on saying it anyway, whispering it against my skin just to make me laugh. I hold him so tight against me, as if that'll keep us here, keep him here with me.

I used to think I was pathetic for thinking soppy, romantic stuff like that. I don't anymore. I just keep thinking it. I keep wanting him here. I keep wanting him to stay.

Afterwards we lie there for a while, Nick's head on my chest and our legs entwined. I reach over to his bedside table and turn the radio on, noticing that it's gone three a.m.—how did that happen? I close my eyes because I think Nick might be asleep, but several

minutes later I hear a click and open my eyes to find he's taken a photo of us lying there, this time on his phone.

"*Nick!*" I grab his phone and check the photo as he laughs gleefully.

"Nothing like a post-sex candid."

I don't reply because I'm just staring at the photo—it's like the ones he took on his disposable camera, natural and unstaged, Nick curled against me and smirking up at the camera, my head leaning on his, my eyes shut and mouth slightly open.

"Don't delete it," says Nick.

"I'm not." I look at it for a second more, and then hand it back to him. "Don't put it on Instagram."

"Can I set it as my wallpaper?"

"What, and get rid of Henry and Nellie? Do you finally love me more than your dogs?"

"Mmm, that's going a bit far . . ."

I roll over, shoving him off me and flipping us so I'm lying on top of him. "Rude."

Nick laughs and wraps his arms around me. "Okay, fine, I love you more than my dogs."

"Good."

"I love you more than anyone, actually."

He says this a little quieter. I move my head out from the crook of his neck so I can meet his eyes.

"Is that weird?" he continues, and then huffs out a small laugh. "I'm only eighteen."

"I don't know," I say. "Maybe."

It is weird. We both know it's weird. We both know *we're* weird, we're not like other couples our age. It's weird that we hang out every single day, it's weird that we'd rather just be with each other all the time. Every day we wonder when we're going to stop feeling like this and get over our teenage relationship. But it never happens. We just keep on going.

Because it's good too. God, it's *so* good.

"I'm weird too," I say, because saying "I love you more than anyone too" back to him doesn't feel quite adequate, even though I honestly love him more than anyone else in the entire world.

Nick squeezes me and says, "Yeah," because he already knows.

NICK

The next morning I wake up to the sound of Charlie's phone alarm and he makes honestly the most adorable grumbling sound I've ever heard, and even though I'm half-asleep I just start laughing. He turns the alarm off and rolls over and asks, "What?" and I'm like, "Don't go to school today. You don't have to go to school ... It's study leave ..." And I reach out my arms and pull him closer to me and he shuts his eyes and mumbles, "Fine."

SOME BONUS EXPLANATION for AMERICAN READERS

Over the years, I've had many questions from American readers about some of the particularly British elements of my stories—for example, sixth form, grammar school, and A-Levels. So for this US edition of Nick and Charlie, my US editor, David Levithan, offered to provide an explanation of the Britishisms that might otherwise require a Google search. Over to you, David!
—AO

To work on the American edition of a British novel is to realize/realise that although we all claim affiliation to the "English language," there are many moments when American and British are, in fact, two separate languages . . . possibly requiring a little translation. The potential for confusion is great: Were Nick and Charlie to head to a Prom at Royal Albert Hall in the springtime, they'd end up at a classical music concert, not a dance. If they were to take out a rubber, it would likely be on the end of a pencil, not to be put on the end of . . . somewhere else. And somehow the fanny means one side of the body on one side of the Atlantic and another side of the body on the other side of the Atlantic, making the placement of a fanny pack a highly disputed notion. The Atlantic has a lot to answer for.

As someone who has spoken fluent American for all my life and has become conversant in British through friends, editing, and—more than anything else—reading books like the one currently in your hands, I would like to offer the following resource for American readers who might be confounded by some of the verbiage they've encountered in Nick and Charlie's story. I concede up front that it might have made more sense to put this aid at the start of the book, before you were inundated with Briticisms. But face it—part of the fun of the experience is trying to master the contextual clues. I assure you that British readers face the same challenges with a novel written in American. *(What are crawdads, and why do they sing? What's the difference between a highway, a freeway, and a turnpike—are they all the same thing? Do Americans really spend their time in fields of rye, catching small children?)*

I will now attempt to walk you through some of the questions that may arise when an American like myself reads *Nick and Charlie*.

Let's start with basic math. Is Year 10 the same thing as 10th grade?

You'd think so, right? Alas, we can't even number our grades the same way. UK schooling starts with something called Reception at age four, which makes it the equivalent of what we call *pre-K*. Then the year that we call kindergarten—which by all rights should be first grade, if you think about it—is Year 1 in the UK. This means that UK years will always be +1 to US grades. This explains the ominously named Year 13 . . . which is actually the rough equivalent of our senior year. I say "rough equivalent" because your next question might be . . .

What's "sixth form" mean?

In a Terry Pratchett novel, the sixth form would no doubt be a nonsensical application you fill out in order to gain adulthood, after having lost the first five forms. But no, sixth form is not an actual form. It's more a function. And it's extra confusing because *it's named after a system that no longer exists.* So the sixth form is no longer the sixth of anything.

But that aside, what is it? The sixth form refers to the final two years of secondary education, aka Years 12 and 13 (or junior and senior year in the States). British students have many different options for their sixth form studies: they can stay at their current school, or move to a different school, or go to a sixth form college, which only caters to students in those final two year groups. Throughout those two final years, students will be usually working toward their A-level exams, but students can also take other academic or vocational courses depending on where they're studying.

So what's an A-level?

This is where it gets really intense, and honestly makes the SATs seem basic. In the two years of the sixth form, you're basically studying for subject-based exams called A-levels. You have to take at least three of them—kind of like choosing which AP classes to take and then spending two whole years focused on those subjects. Subjects include English Language & Literature, Maths—

Sorry to interrupt, but is that a typo? Don't you mean "Math"?

UK logic says that we're shortening "Mathematics" here and, if you shorten a plural, it should stay plural, thank you very much. US logic says there's only one Math, just like there's one Science or one Literature when you're talking about a general field. I do not have the diplomatic skills to reconcile these logics, so we're going to have to agree to disagree on this one.

Now, as I was saying . . . subjects for A-levels include English Language & Literature, Maths, Biology, Physics, Chemistry, History, Geography, Psychology, Economics, Art, Information Technology, Photography, and languages such as French, German, and Spanish. You take one big exam with each subject as its own module, and then get a score from an A to an E. (Good news: You can't get an F!) Sadistically, if you bomb on one of the subjects and want to take the exam over, you can't just take that one subject/module over—you have to take the whole thing over again. Your coursework in these subjects is also part of your A-level grade.

I imagine this is all rather stressful. You can see why Nick may be on edge. Universities and many employers look at your A levels when you apply for school, jobs, or apprenticeships.

If, after you graduate high school, you want to continue your schooling, you go to college, right?

No! Word choice again causes confusion here. In the UK, *college* and *university* are not used interchangeably the way they are in the US. In the UK, if you head off to college, you are doing your sixth form (Years 12 and 13!) in a different institution than where you had your secondary schooling. In American terms, you're doing college prep in . . . something called college. Then, when your two years are done and you're a-levels are completed, you head to university. (A university may have individual colleges within it, but that's a different use of the word *college* and I don't want to get into it here, for fear of confusing you even more.)

So if a sixteen-year-old Brit tells me they're in college . . .

. . . it doesn't mean they're a prodigy and graduated from high school two years early. It just means that they're doing their university-prep coursework (i.e., junior and senior year) at a school that's different from their secondary school.

If you had to take an A-level exam based on the British education system, do you think you'd pass?

No, I do not think I would. I think I would get an E.

I'm also confused when teen characters say they're going to grammar school. That sounds like they've been held back, right?

It sounds that way to American ears, but is not the case. In the UK, *grammar school* is not a synonym for *elementary school*. A grammar school in the UK is what we might think of as a magnet school here in the US. They are state secondary schools that you can apply to when you're eleven (another exam!). According to the BBC, of some three thousand state secondary schools in England, only 163 are grammar schools. Scotland, Wales, and many counties in England don't have grammar schools at all. (It's important to note that although I'm using the term *UK* throughout this explanation, there are wild regional divergences for much of what I'm saying within the UK—I once had a five-city UK book tour, and in each city I went to, when I told people where I'd been, they exclaimed, "Oh, the accent in [that city]! I can't understand a word they're saying!" These cities were, at most, six hours apart.)

An example of a question you might be asked to get into a grammar school is this:

Maggie Smith, Judi Dench, Ian McKellen, Helen Mirren, and Angela Lansbury are out shopping for jumpers. Helen Mirren and Judi Dench want patterned jumpers, Ian McKellen and Angela Lansbury want brightly colored jumpers with hoods, Judi Dench and Maggie Smith want lightweight jumpers, and Maggie Smith and Helen Mirren want brightly colored jumpers but with an extra-warm lining.

Out of the following statements, which one must be true?

A. Angela Lansbury and Ian McKellen want different types of jumpers.

B. Only two people do not want brightly colored jumpers.

C. No one wants a lightweight jumper with a hood.

D. Angela Lansbury wants a jumper with a hood and a warm lining.

E. Four of them do not want patterned jumpers.

Shall we talk about something less complicated? Like . . . football?

This is like the holy grail of the American/British disconnect. And, frankly, with this one, the Brits seem to have rationality on their side. The sport that's played mostly with your feet? That's probably the one that should be called *football*. The one where, yeah, your feet do some running work, but they're not really the star of the show? Probably not the prime candidate to be called *football*.

But just in case you're curious: What we Americans call soccer got that name because it was called association football in the UK, as a way to delineate it from rugby football. Association = assoc = soc = soccer.

Association football and rugby football had a hot, steamy encounter, bore a child, and said, "Well, since football is your last name and it's also my last name, let's just call the fruit of our union by that last name." Hence, American football was born. And once it became popular, there was no going back—it was association football that needed to change its name.

Now, why is American football a much bigger sport than American soccer when it comes to pro leagues, even though more kids actually play soccer? Let's just say capitalism, and move on to the next question.

(Also, the answer for the above test question is C.)

I understand why a wool garment I put on my top half is called a sweater, because I get all sweaty when I wear it. But in the UK it's called a jumper. Why is this? Are sweaters much itchier there?

Probably. But that's not the reason it's called a jumper. Jumper-as-sweater derives from the French *jupe*, for a short coat. So blame the French—the British often do.

Okay, pop quiz. Can you explain the following?

Biscuit hour.

In the UK, a biscuit is a cookie. So biscuit hour is clearly a time to eat cookies. I doubt it takes a whole hour. (Side note: My friend Gabriel, who is as British as Paddington, had never heard of biscuit hour, and neither had his friends. I would like to think this is a sly effort on Alice Oseman's part to spread the concept so that soon everyone in the UK will be taking an hour to sit around and eat biscuits.)

Crisps.

It's a slippery slope here. Crisps in the UK are chips in the US, whereas chips in the UK are fries in the US.

Car park.

Not, alas, a place where cars go for a stroll, to take in some foliage, maybe play Frisbee on a hot summer day. A car park is a parking lot.

Pavement.

A 1990s indie band that I never liked as much as I thought I should. Also, in the UK it's a sidewalk, whereas in the US it's the substance that makes up the street. In other musical terms, when Adele sings that she's chasing pavements, it doesn't mean that she's in love with the art of road making. She just can't stop walking on the sidewalks of life.

Oreo Dairy Milk Bar (aka Cadbury Dairy Milk Oreo).

If the Amazon reviews are to believed, this candy is heaven condensed into a solid form. You would think that UK and US chocolate would be the same . . . but no! US chocolate is usually sweeter, with sugar as the first ingredient. UK chocolate, however, prioritizes the cow over the cane and makes milk its first ingredient. In this case, that milky chocolate is mixed with bits of Oreo cookie, then sold in bar form. At least one Amazon reviewer recommends eating it chilled for maximum pleasure.

Tombola.

Um . . . Thomas Bola's nickname. No? (Quickly looks something up.) Oh! It's the Italian word for a raffle. Which Brits apparently like as much as the English word for raffle. Only . . . it's not exactly the same as a raffle. As I have been told by someone in the know, in a raffle, you buy a ticket that is put into a hat for a draw at a later point in the hope of winning a corresponding prize, whereas a tombola will be a table full of numbered prizes (usually either bottles of wine or toys) and a hat full of tickets. You pull your own ticket out and either win or lose on the spot, depending on whether there's a number on it or not. Aren't you glad you asked? Are you rushing off to a village fete to try your luck? I personally would like to invent a tombaffle, where, after you put your name into a hat, bottles of wine and toys pay good money for a chance to take you home.

End of pop quiz. Now, if I sent you a text that said, *You gotta help me, David—Ignatius is really pissed*, what would you advise?

If Ignatius is American, I would advise you ask him what's wrong, and to try to work out the source of his anger, because if Ignatius is American and pissed, he's angry. However, if Ignatius is British, I would advise that you tell him to: drink lots of water, not operate a vehicle, and don't even think about texting any of his exes. Because if he's British and pissed, that means he's drunk drunk *drunk*. (But if you tell him this, he may get pissed off—a phrase that is the same in all regions.)

I need some new fashionable footwear—I should head to Boots, right?

Only if you want to be wearing a foot brace to your next gala! Strangely, you won't find any boots at Boots; it is a big pharmacy chain, like CVS or Walgreens. (It is named after its founder, John Boot.) For footwear, you could go to Schuh, which when pronounced by an American will probably come out like the sound you make when you get off the couch after sitting on it for twelve hours.

Is a box fort a fort made of boxes?

Actually, it is.

Are fairy lights made from real fairies?

Only in England. In America, we tend to think they're made by elves and call them Christmas lights. Even in July.

Can you explain rounders to me?

It's a game involving a bat and bases and a ball, but it's not baseball. You should probably just look this one up online for the nuances.

How about "chucking it down"?

When it rains real hard in America, we invoke cats and dogs. When it rains real hard in the UK, they reference some guy named Chuck. Which, come to think of it, is a nickname for Charles . . . or Charlie. This bears further investigation.

I hope this conversation has helped you as much as it's helped me, and will inform all your further reading about Nick, Charlie, and their friends. I'm off now to change my jumper so I can get a game of rounders in before biscuit hour is through!

Nick Nelson

FULL NAME
Nicholas Nelson

AGE
18

SCHOOL YEAR
Year 13

BIRTHDAY
September 4th

LIKES
- rugby
- dogs
- baking

DISLIKES
- horror movies
- bugs
- bullies

Charlie Spring

FULL NAME
Charles Francis Spring

AGE
17

SCHOOL YEAR
Year 12

BIRTHDAY
April 27th

LIKES
- music
- Nick's hoodies
- naps

DISLIKES
- no wifi
- being cold
- bad mental health days